Better than She Deserved

Better than She Deserved

A Willow Hall Sequel

LEENIE BROWN

LEENIE B BOOKS
HALIFAX

Cover design by Leenie B Books. Images sourced from Deposit Photos and Period Images.

Contents

Dedication

To the many readers on my blog
and at darcyandlizzy.com
who wished to know what happened to
Caroline after she left Pemberley
and
to Julie and Patty,
whose suggestions on a blog post,
resulted in a name for our hero

Prelude

Dear Readers,

Below is an excerpt from *At All Cost*, which is book 4 of Willow Hall a Pride and Prejudice Variation Series. If you have not had the opportunity to read this novel yet, you may find the following passage beneficial since the rumours started here as Caroline strolls around Pemberley's garden with Captain Harris are referenced several times in *Better Than She Deserved*.

Happy Reading,

Leenie B.

~*~*~

Caroline accepted the arm of Captain Harris when he offered to escort her on a stroll.

"I have heard your name mentioned," said Harris

as they began their walk, "and I am most happy to now have made your acquaintance. The militia has kept me away, you see."

"You said your father lives near here?" Caroline asked as she studied his features. Captain Harris was nearly a head taller than she was, and his shoulders were wide while his waist was narrow. The arm on which her hand rested was firm, and she guessed him to be very strong. His hair fell around his ears in wisps of golden brown, and his face was angular but not harshly so. Overall, he was quite attractive, but looks were not the salient point when judging a gentleman. No matter the perfection of the physical specimen, it was his accounts and holdings that truly defined his worth to Caroline.

"He does. Not six miles from Aldwood Abbey. Mr. Dobney is my uncle — my mother's sister was his wife." He glanced down at Caroline. "Have you been to Aldwood Abbey?"

"Yes, once."

"Well, then, I shall compare my father's estate with it since you might remember how large Aldwood Abbey is?"

"Oh, I remember every estate I visit. I am very

good at that sort of thing. I admire architecture and finishings, you see. The way they lead the eye and present themselves is of great interest to me. So much can be said of a man and his character just by the state of his garden."

She hoped from the smile he favoured her with that he understood her meaning. She would not even consider a man without a proper estate that was well-tended. There were areas where appearances were important, and the impressing of callers, the care of a garden, the right drapery and paintings, and a proper placement of furniture must all be considered as necessities.

"I quite agree, and should you ever visit my father's home, you would find gardens as fine as these," he waved his hand toward the garden, "they lack only size in comparison. My mother has a fine eye, and father dotes on her — though not to extravagance." He shook his head. "Oh, no, Father is far from extravagant."

"So your father's estate is well-tended?"

Harris nodded. "Yes, quite. But, we digress. I was to describe to you the size of the estate."

Caroline looked at him eagerly. He seemed to possess a proper understanding of the importance of appearances and holdings. In fact, he seemed to be a man who would use his money wisely to increase his standing, and she found this fact to be almost as attractive as his face — and the longer she looked at him, the more she had to admit that his face was handsome.

"The lands attached to my father's estate are equal to those of Aldwood Abbey, but we have a greater number of fields, and an attached farm to the west that is let out...but land holdings are not what most ladies find of interest about the estate." He again smiled down at her. "As I said the gardens are magnificent, but the house — ah, there is the true beauty of the estate. The house shines like a jewel surrounded by its gardens and backed by the stand of woods. The drive is not so long as the one here, but there is ample time when a carriage is spotted at the turn for tea to be ordered before the guests arrive at the door. And then, well — my mother's eye is as good at interiors as it is at exteriors. The rooms, and there are only two fewer than at Aldwood Abbey– we have no chapel or chapel anteroom — are so well furnished in a traditional classical style. If you were to be visiting longer, I would insist that you come visit. I am certain you would not be disappointed."

"I dare say you are correct! You have described such a place as I would find every pleasure in seeing. Tell me, what were the impressions of the Bennets on seeing it?"

"Oh, I could not say. I have yet to persuade them to visit."

There was a distinct note of disappointment in his tone that did not evade Caroline's notice. Perhaps, Captain Harris might prove handy in creating a trying environment for Miss Eliza to be entering.

"Do not tell me," Caroline cried, "that Miss Bennet and Miss Elizabeth limit themselves to Pemberley when there are estates such as your father's to visit!"

"No, no. They divide their time between here, the Abbey, and Kympton."

Caroline's brows rose. Was Jane attempting to ensnare Marcus Dobey? "They visit Aldwood Abbey?"

Harris nodded. "Their sister is to marry my cousin Marcus, so it is only natural that they would."

"Miss Bennet is to marry Mr. Marcus Dobney?" she asked in surprise.

Harris laughed. "No, Miss Lydia is to marry Marcus."

"Miss Lydia?" Caroline's eyes grew wide, and her brows rose.

Harris chuckled again. "It is quite the story how it came to be."

"Indeed?"

Harris's lips curled upward slyly as he nodded.

"Do tell," Caroline encouraged.

And he did.

Caroline could not believe what she was hearing. Such tales that could be shared! Oh, the pleasure of tickling Louisa's ears in the carriage! The thought was nearly enough for her to wish to leave that moment, but one must not ignore an opportunity to add to succulent secrets.

"I should say I am surprised, I suppose," Caroline peeked up at him with a coquettish smile and flutter of lashes, "but I am not. The way the Bennets present themselves in public!" She gasped and shook her head. "Oh, the eldest girls present themselves quite well, but the mother and the younger girls — it is quite embarrassing."

"I have no doubt," said Harris. "Miss Lydia was the most determined flirt in Brighton. I heard rumors that she was not ungenerous with her charms."

Oh, this was the opening that Caroline had longed for! A place where she might be able to see Jane and Elizabeth lowered as they should be. And so, she leaned closer and whispered, "I should not say this since he is my brother, but you seem the sort of person who can be trusted." She looked at Harris and waited for the agreement that was not long in coming. "Miss Bennet and Miss Eliza stayed at Netherfield, the estate my brother leased in Hertfordshire, for several days. I cannot say for certain, but there were whispers amongst the staff that not everything was proper."

"Do you mean, Miss Bennet or Miss Elizabeth was not proper?" He asked in surprise.

"I know it is shocking," Caroline agreed. "I cannot say it was one or the other — some things are best left unsaid. However, I can tell you that Miss Bennet was whisked away to her aunt's home only a little more than a month thereafter, and, well, Mr. Darcy is excessively enamoured with Miss Elizabeth, so…" she let the story end there as Harris's eyes grew wide.

"But your brother is not engaged to Miss Bennet. Is his honor not injured by not offering for her?"

Caroline shrugged. "I do not know that my brother did not offer and was rejected. Nor do I know if he found her — hmmm," she tapped her lips with her finger, "untouched. Miss Bennet smiles very easily at all the men she meets."

They walked along in silence for a few strides. "I fear I have fallen prey to her smiles," Harris finally admitted, "but she seemed so decorous."

"That she does," Caroline said sadly. "I, of course, broke off my friendship with her as soon as I knew."

"As you should!" declared Harris, "And as I will."

"You will not say anything about what I have shared, will you? She is a woman in need of a good home at some point. Her father is not well to do."

Harris looked toward the house that was now just before them. "I shall not whisper a word," he assured her.

Caroline thanked him but knew that this secret

would not stay hidden. How could it? It was tantalizing. Miss Bennet would not succeed with any gentleman in Derbyshire, and Charles? She shrugged mentally. It was possible that his reputation might come into question, but he was a man and as such, indiscretions were forgivable. However, she thought as a smile curled her lips, if it did hurt him, it was no more than he deserved for first, ruining her chances with Darcy and then, turning her away from Pemberley to sleep at an inn.

Chapter 1

Caroline Bingley stared at her sister's husband. He could not be serious! Choose a husband at this house party?

"If you are unsuccessful here, your brother says you may have a season to secure a match, but after that, you will either set up your own establishment or go to live with your aunt in Manchester." Fredrick Hurst lowered the letter he had been reading and glared at Caroline. "I told you we should not have gone to Pemberley. But would you listen?"

He rose from the chair in the library at Burton Hall which he had commandeered for this meeting with his wife's trying younger sister. "You have always wanted to have your way. You think nothing of anyone else. How many times did Charles tell you that Darcy would not have you? But did you listen?"

Caroline cowered slightly in her chair. Hurst was never so vocal about his displeasure. Normally, he would scowl and mutter, but rarely did he raise his voice.

"Have you no words to rebuff me?" Hurst stood above her. "Or will you spread rumours about me as well? Perhaps you could share with one and all that your sister has not yet had a child because..." He scratched his chin and pursed his lips as he thought of a plausible and scandalous reason. "Oh, I know. It is because I spend all my nights with a mistress instead of my wife — which is no less true than what you have said about others."

Caroline's eyes grew wide as he leaned toward her. "I would never –"

"No," Hurst cut her off. "You will not speak until I am well and truly through with you. I have put up with your antics for your sister's sake for these three years, but I will not do so any longer. "

He waved the letter he held in his hand an inch from her face. "Your brother? You would accuse your brother of such ungentlemanly behaviour as seducing and leaving Miss Bennet, who, I might add, you claimed as a friend! Not to mention what you have said about Darcy and Miss Elizabeth!"

He turned from Caroline in disgust and shook his head as he gave an exasperated sigh. "No, you will marry before the season begins if I have to affect a compromise to guarantee it."

He turned back toward her. "I do not wish to host you for a season." He flicked the letter with his finger. "Charles is too good. I would have sent you off to your aunt in Manchester without a farthing of your money for what you did."

Again, Caroline cowered under his glower. She had heard stories from Hurst's friends that he was not a man with whom to trifle, but she had never seen it until now.

"You will go to your room and remain there until it is time to gather for dinner. And then, you will appear and be as sweet to everyone as you are when you are pretending to care about Darcy or his sister."

He studied her for a moment. His anger with Caroline was only slightly cooled, and he was determined to impress upon her just how grievous her actions had been. He shrugged. Perhaps it might be beneficial if she were to be treated in a similar fashion to those she ridiculed.

"You are not without your charms, I suppose. Your complexion is good. Your teeth fine. Your eyes are acceptable, though unremarkable, and your nose is perfectly straight. Your maid is clearly adept at styling your hair to best suit your features, and the modiste, though she listens to your preference for colors — which are only marginally flattering — does know how to drape your assets to best advantage." He bit back a smile at her horrified expression.

"And if all that is not effective, you do have twenty thousand pounds. I am certain there is at least one man here who would welcome such a sum." Hurst shrugged again. "I would not be averse to throwing in a few extra quid if need be." He waved to the door. "To your room," he instructed. "And do come to dinner ready to win a man's admiration."

Caroline opened her mouth to speak.

"No," he answered before she could utter a sound. "I have changed my mind. Even though I am through with you for the moment, I find I do not wish to hear what you have to say. There is no way you can explain away what you have done."

Caroline snapped her mouth shut, and her eyes narrowed.

"Do not even contemplate retaliation, dear sister," Hurst warned. "For if you do, I assure you, I will see you on the first coach bound for Manchester. " He waved once more toward the door, and Caroline, having no other recourse, did as instructed and rose to retire to her room.

~*~*~

Mr. Franklin Rhett slipped down the hall and away from the over-zealous matrons in the drawing room. Even though he lacked an estate and his fortune was acquired from both his father, who was a manufacturer, and an uncle on his mother's side, who was in trade, he was not being ignored as he had expected he would be. He chuckled to himself. No, the ladies and their chaperones were far from ignoring him. It was quite the opposite. He had been interviewed — or as the ladies would phrase it, engaged in conversation — by at least three chaperones before he had made his escape. There were two others, who, while talking to some of the other gentlemen in the room, had been eying him as if he were a platter of sweets.

However, Rhett was more interested in finding his friend and having a discussion of some importance with him instead of entertaining the marriage-hungry mob in the drawing room. If he knew Hurst — and he knew him quite well — Hurst would likely be in the library with a glass of brandy or port. If there was one thing that man knew how to do, other than making money, it was finding a place that would provide a fortifying beverage and a safe haven from females.

Rhett could feel the tension of the past several minutes melting from his shoulders as the voices from the other room faded with each step he took toward the library. He heaved a great sigh of relief as he neared his destination and was just reaching for the knob of the door through which lay his escape to solitude and manly machinations when it opened, and he was presented with a delightful surprise. He smiled and made no move to make way for the ball of fury who was propelling her way through the door.

Caroline was so infuriated with her brother-in-law's high-handedness and so determined to close the door behind her in such a way as to signal her displeasure that she did not bother to look where she was going. And, so, having pulled the door to with a resounding bang, she turned and bumped straight into a very solid masculine figure. "Oh," she gasped as she stumbled backward.

"Are you well?" Rhett asked as he caught Caroline by the elbow, helping her keep her footing.

"Yes, yes, I am well. Thank you," Caroline muttered.

She was well as far has her person went, but where her happiness was concerned, she was far from well. She had failed at securing the position of mistress of Pemberley, and now, her funds were being cut to an alarmingly low level, and her sister's husband, who was supposed to be easily swayed, was giving her two weeks to find a husband. Two weeks!

She huffed at the thought. It was only a bit of gossip which she had started. Yet, Hurst acted as if she had desecrated some hallowed place. She smoothed her sleeves and checked her gown. Well, it was perhaps rather scandalous gossip.

"I am glad you are unscathed, Miss Bingley." Rhett's lips remained curled into a pleased smile.

This was the lady he had hoped to find at this house party. In fact, it was only because Hurst had mentioned being forced to escort his wife's sister to this party that Rhett had retrieved his own discarded invitation and accepted against his first inclination.

Caroline's brows furrowed as she studied the face of the man in front of her. He looked familiar, but she could not place his name. He was a friend of Hurst, she believed, or at least, he was a gentleman who sought Hurst's advice about investments. Of course, that meant he was not the sort of man to whom she would have paid attention as she rarely spared a thought about friends of Hurst. It also indicated that this gentleman was likely no better off in his societal standing than she was. And if a gentleman was not the smallest step above Caroline in social standing, she had no time for him — even if he was as handsome as the one standing in front of her.

"Mr. Franklin Rhett," he said by way of introduction. "I believe we have met at a few soirees and in passing when I visited your brother."

Caroline curtseyed and smiled as was proper. "I must apologize. I do not recall our meeting." She was happy to have placed him as a friend of Hurst, but she dearly wished she remembered their meeting so that she would know more about him, for he was rather captivating with those piercing blue eyes and raven black locks that fell softly on his forehead and hung around his ears.

"That is to be expected, I suppose, as I was never fortunate enough to secure a dance," he paused, "although I did make an attempt." He stepped to the side to let her pass but caught her arm as she did. "I do hope we can at least spend a few moments getting to know one another while we are here. I know there is no dancing for a fortnight, but perhaps you would join me for a walk in the garden one day?"

"Perhaps," she replied, pulling her arm away gently. There was something very unsettling about both the way he looked at her and his touch. It was not unpleasantly unsettling, but unsettling nonetheless. She glanced over her shoulder as she scurried down the hall. She would have to ask her sister about Mr. Rhett. If he were of good standing, perhaps he could take Mr. Darcy's place. Not that any estate, she admitted with a sigh, could ever compare to Pemberley.

~*~*~

"Ah, Hurst, I thought I might find you here." Rhett entered the library and nodded his acceptance when Hurst lifted the decanter of port in offer of a glass. "I met your sister in the hall. She did not look pleased."

Hurst laughed. "She is not, but then again, neither am I — nor is Bingley. Caroline has pushed her ambitions too far this time."

Rhett's brows rose. "Indeed?" This sounded promising.

"Do not get me started," Hurst said as he handed his friend a glass before taking his own and dropping into a chair. "Darcy is marrying."

Ah, so that was it. "And he is not marrying her?"

There were not many who were unaware of Caroline Bingley's ambitions in regards to Mr. Fitzwilliam Darcy.

Hurst laughed once again. "As if that were ever a possibility." He shook his head as he continued to chuckle. "No, he is not marrying Caroline. Darcy found a country miss." He smirked and lifted a brow as he made the statement. "Miss Elizabeth Bennet of Longbourn in Hertfordshire is a gentleman's daughter, but not one of significance. Mr.

Bennet's estate stands next to Netherfield, you see."

"The place your sister did not wish her brother to take?"

Hurst tapped his nose as he swallowed a large amount of his port. "Precisely." He placed his nearly empty glass on the table beside him. "It gets worse."

"Worse than losing Darcy to a country nobody because her brother took Netherfield against her better judgment?" Rhett asked with a laugh.

"Charles is marrying Miss Elizabeth's sister Jane."

Rhett's eyes grew wide. "And then Bingley shall remain forever at this estate his sister despises?"

Hurst shook his head. "It is unlikely. Miss Bennet and Miss Elizabeth are close. I suspect Charles will be looking for something in Derbyshire. But it is enough that he is marrying the sister of the lady who dashed all of Caroline's aspirations. Caroline attempted to prevent Charles from attaching himself to Miss Bennet, of course, but she has only been successful in being cut off."

A pleased smile crept across Rhett's face. Things appeared to be very promising.

"I have given her until the end of this blasted party to secure a husband."

Rhett drained the last of his port from his glass. "So, you would be open to negotiations?"

Hurst blinked. "You would wish to take that," he waved at the door through which Caroline had recently exited, "for a wife?"

"I assure you all my mental faculties are functioning as they should be," Rhett said in response to the incredulous look Hurst was giving him. "I find her attractive, and before she set her cap at Darcy, she was pleasant, even charming and witty at times."

Hurst cleared his throat. "Your money comes from manufacturing,"

Rhett nodded. "Which is why she has refused to dance with me twice if I recall correctly." He held up a finger. "And I believe, it was your wife who reminded her of my disqualifications."

Hurst grimaced. "Louisa is far too willing to do anything to keep her sister happy." He returned to his drink. "That is why I have given Caroline until the end of this party to engage herself to some man. I cannot abide the thought of hosting her for the season." He raised a brow. "Especially on limited funds from Charles."

So Hurst was not exaggerating when he said the chit had been cut off. "Her dowry remains as it was?"

Hurst nodded. "But you are still not landed gentry."

Rhett shrugged. "Not yet, but I am not opposed to taking an estate. You know this." He leaned forward. "As I see it, my friend, you have a problem with which I can help."

Hurst shook his head. He wished to see Caroline out the door and into someone else's home, but he was confident she would not be easily convinced to accept anything less than a gentleman in possession of money and an estate. She was desperate to leave her ties to trade behind. "I do not see her even entertaining the thought."

Rhett's smile grew. "That does not need to be a hindrance. If you wished to make a deal with a chap who was being difficult, how would you go about it?"

The question was met by a short burst of laughter. "I would remove all other options." Hurst tipped his head and looked at his friend. Rhett was not a weak-willed man. He might do very well for Caroline. "You would take on such a surly wife?"

"I would, though I would do my best to help her return to the lady she was before she set her cap at Darcy." Rhett settled back into this chair and unbuttoned his waistcoat. "Now, tell me what she has done to push an amiable man like Charles to the point of cutting her off, and I shall devise a plan to secure her as the wife I desire."

Chapter 2

Caroline sighed and ran a finger along the top of the small round table that stood near the window as she crossed from her bed to the window. Her room was beautiful even if it was not spacious. The shades of blue were calming. She pulled her feet up under her skirts as she settled onto the cushions of the window seat in such a way that she could see a portion of the garden which lay just beyond the corner of the house.

Burton Hall, Mr. Hadaway's estate, was not without merit. The gardens were pleasing, and the house itself was large enough to comfortably hold the dozen or so young gentlemen and ladies as well as the chaperones who were in attendance at the party. Every room which Caroline had seen was decorated in a tasteful, if slightly older, fashion. It was not Pemberley, but being mistress of Burton Hall would not be without some prestige.

She wrapped her arms around her legs and rested her chin on her knees while she considered the unmarried owner of Burton Hall. Mr. Hadaway was perhaps a touch on the older side of acceptable being just past five and thirty, and he was not exactly the most handsome or fit gentleman she had ever met. He could only complete one set of dances before becoming winded, and his girth was not so large as to be portly, though it was by no means thin. He was not particularly the sort of gentleman she would be drawn to in a ballroom, but his home was lovely and had been in his family for several generations.

She straightened as the door opened and her sister entered.

"You are allowed to see me?" Caroline's tone was bitter. "I am surprised your husband has not banned you from doing so."

"Why ever should Hurst do such a thing?" Louisa crossed the room and joined Caroline on the window seat. "I have come with a list of names and qualifications." She sighed. "I know how much you wished to marry Mr. Darcy, but since that is not to be, we must find you the next best thing."

Caroline expelled a rush of air. "I suppose you are correct." She took the list of names from her sister. "Which of these gentleman should I choose?"

"Oh, there are a couple who are quite eligible," Louisa answered, "but one must not rush things. There is still the season."

Caroline laughed bitterly. "No, there is not. Your husband has given me until the end of this party to find a husband."

Louisa blinked. "Hurst has done what?"

Caroline's smile was tight. "Apparently, your husband feels my little disparagements of our brother and the Miss Bennets to be highly disagreeable."

Louisa bit her lip. "They were rather harsh."

Caroline rolled her eyes. Louisa had never had the stomach to be as fully a part of the devious world of matchmaking and husband-snaring of the ton as Caroline had been. It was fortunate that Louisa had found a good match so easily.

"It is no more than one might hear whispered about Almacks," Caroline argued. "Everyone knows it is not true — or at least not completely true." She shrugged. "It was merely a discouragement to Captain Harris."

It had been more than that, of course. Caroline had wanted Jane and Elizabeth Bennet to be looked upon with reproach. It was what simple country girls deserved for attempting to reach so high as Pemberley.

"I am not convinced it was necessary to malign our own brother in such a salacious fashion," scolded Louisa, "and I should think, Mr. Darcy, with his aversion to all things disreputable, will find he needs very little reason to cut you from his sphere of friends. Charles had already laid the groundwork for such a thing before we visited Pemberley on our way here. And you know as well as I that one cut from Mr. Darcy in any of the ballrooms in London will surely limit your acceptability, and we must remember that our parents were not of the ton."

Caroline knew what her sister was saying was true. The Bingley name only carried any weight within polite society due to their connection with Mr. Darcy. That was a fact she should have, perhaps, considered more carefully before exacting her revenge on her brother and the Bennets. However, it did rankle to have to admit one's sister was correct.

"I will admit you may be right. Mr. Darcy can be very high and mighty."

Louisa raised a brow. "You spoke poorly of the woman who will be his wife."

"Not that she should be," muttered Caroline.

Louisa blew out a breath. "My dear sister, I know you will not listen, but I am going to say it anyway. The heart will want what the heart wants and often without consideration for wealth and standing. I was fortunate to find a man of a proper position who also engaged my heart, and I engaged his."

"You know Aunt has always said I should marry well to lift our family from its roots," Caroline returned.

Louisa pursed her lips as if she wished to say more but dared not.

Caroline smiled sweetly at her sister. "I should not wish to disappoint Aunt," Caroline said with a bat of her lashes. "Now, tell me which of these men I should consider first."

She ran her finger down the list stopping at the name of the intriguing man she had met in the hall outside the library. "What do you know of Mr. Rhett?"

"Oh, he is very handsome," said Louisa with a small giggle. "Dark hair, blue eyes, wide shoulders." She sighed. "And he is pleasant if a bit sharp and intense at times. I have met him, you see, on several occasions as he is friends with Hurst. However, he does not have an estate, although he does have a nice home in London and is much like our brother in having been left a great deal of money. Do you not remember him?"

Caroline shook her head. He looked so familiar. Surely, she should be able to remember a gentleman as handsome as Mr. Rhett.

"His money comes from manufacturing much like our father's, and a portion, at least, of his relations reside in Manchester. That is where you first met him. I say the boy was smitten with you. He attempted to dance with you when you were just fifteen when Aunt had allowed us to attend a gathering at," she paused and tapped her lip. "Oh, I cannot remember her name, but she had the worst taste in design I ever saw."

"Mrs. Taggart?"

"Yes! That is it exactly! Aunt would not have

allowed us to attend except the lady had a relation somewhere along the line that was a cousin or some such to an earl, and she wished for us to practice our dancing so that we would be ready for the all-important season in London."

"I remember that soiree, but I do not remember Mr. Rhett."

Louisa laughed. "Oh, he looked nothing as he does now, that is for certain. A bit awkward and gangly, but his smile was pleasant."

"And I did not dance with him?"

Louisa shook her head. "No. He was from manufacturing, and Aunt would have scolded you most severely."

Caroline remembered her aunt's scolding. It was loud and long and oft-repeated. One was not allowed to forget an offense. It was why Caroline had learned quickly to shun all but the best in society. Her own kind was to be left behind, for Caroline and Louisa were destined for something better than being a tradesman's wife.

"He also sought you out during your first season, near the end, after I was betrothed to Hurst, and Charles had introduced us to Darcy."

"He did?"

Louisa lifted a brow. "You gave him a cut, dear sister. Do you not remember? I whispered to you about a gentleman who kept looking at you and who was approaching. You inquired who he was, and I said a friend of Hurst. You asked his situation. I told you of his fortune from trade, and you turned from him as he approached and walked away?"

"That was him?" Caroline had not given the gentleman more than a passing glance. Features were of little significance when fortune was not what it should be. However, after having met the gentleman earlier, she was not altogether certain features did not require greater consideration. Perhaps if he were to purchase an estate, then he would be a true gentleman, not of long-standing, mind you, but enough of one to not disappoint her aunt.

"Does he intend to purchase an estate?" Caroline asked.

While a more established gentleman might be a better option, Caroline could not deny that the idea of choosing her own home rather than moving into one that she might not like so well or might be in the entirely wrong part of the country did not have its advantages. She would likely be able to guarantee that it was close to town, which would be preferable, of course. Country life was so dull unless one was hosting a gathering.

"That I do not know," Louisa said. "He came into his fortune four years ago, so he has had ample time to secure an estate and yet has not. I think he prefers the activity of London, and when the summer comes, he often travels to the sea though I do not know exactly where."

Caroline considered that for a few moments. The idea that Mr. Rhett preferred town was a mark in his favour. However, he still lacked the all-important quality of an estate. She shrugged. "He must have an estate or at the very least, be interested in obtaining one, which it sounds as if he is not." With a pang of disappointment, she mentally crossed Mr. Rhett off her list

"He may be interested once he finds a wife. Men often become more serious once they begin considering wives and heirs and all that." Louisa smiled. "I should not discount him entirely. He is Hurst's friend so we would be often together."

Caroline nodded. "Very well, I shall keep him at the bottom of the list." It would be pleasant to travel in the same circle of intimate acquaintances as her sister. "Now, who should be at the top? Mr. Hadaway?"

Louisa wrinkled her nose and shook her head. "No, your children would not be pretty, and his mother," she rolled her eyes, "so demanding! I have heard tell that she has run off three prospective candidates already." Louisa shook her head again. "No. I would not wish to visit you if she were your mother-in-law. You know how I do not like disagreeable women."

It was true. Louisa disliked disagreement of any sort. It was a quality that Caroline had used to her advantage many times over the years.

"But Burton Hall..."

"No," Louisa interrupted. "This estate is not worth that sort of unpleasantness. Now, Mr. Pritchard has an excellent estate south of London, which had been in his family for several generations." She screwed up her face as she thought. "I believe it is within a day and a half's drive of town. So, it is not so very far that travel is difficult, especially with his fine carriage and horses. He has exquisite taste, and no mother to be a bother. He also has a home in Mayfair and, well, he is very easy to admire." She waggled her brows. "There are not many finer figures here, save for, perhaps, Mr. Rhett."

And so the conversation continued, down the list, gentleman by gentleman, until all six men had been evaluated.

Caroline studied the list for a moment longer after her sister had finished. That name Franklin Rhett stood out, but with a sigh, she ignored it and said instead, "Mr. Pritchard shall have to do."

"He will be in demand," Louisa cautioned. "And Hurst is already displeased with you, so you will need to tread carefully. Your usual tactics will not work."

Caroline smiled brightly. "You forget, dear sister, that I am capable of being delightfully pleasant."

Louisa did not look convinced but said nothing. Instead, she rose and opened the wardrobe. "Which shall you wear this evening?"

Caroline tilted her head to one side and then the other. "The green one. It is very flattering." No matter what Hurst might have said.

"A good choice," said Louisa, pulling it out and

then ringing the bell to have the maid come to help Caroline get ready.

~*~*~

Rhett pulled at his sleeves and stretched his lips around in a circle preparing for the hours of smiling that were to begin with this short gathering before dinner and carry on until the matrons had decided their charges had displayed their accomplishments and batted their lashes enough for one evening. He shook his head. Finding a wife with whom one could share a happy life in such a sea of insincerity was — he sighed — impossible, really. Honesty and directness were much more favorable to such pretense.

He sighed again before stepping into the ornately decorated drawing room and the den of ravenous chaperones who saw his looks and demeanor to some extent but looked more to his bank accounts than his person. And, well, his accounts were very handsome. He smiled.

"Good evening, Mrs. Whimple. Both you and your charge are looking fetching this evening," Rhett greeted a grey-haired lady with a round figure and a friendly face. The young lady standing next to her, blushed as she had likely been schooled to do in the presence of a gentleman.

"Charlotte is a gem, but then, I am rather partial to her." Mrs. Whimple pushed the girl, of whom she was so fond, forward. "Charlotte, this is Mr. Rhett. Mr. Rhett, my niece, Miss Whimple."

"A pleasure to meet you." Rhett did what was proper and bowed over the hand the chit had extended to him. "I trust you are finding Burton Hall to your liking? It is a grand home and well-furnished."

"It is a lovely home, and our room is very comfortable." Charlotte Whimple smiled, looked down, and then peered up at him from under her lashes as she replied.

It was a ploy Rhett found particularly off-putting. It was supposed to display demureness, but to him, it signalled a lady who was rather scheming. But then, that was the reason he had come to speak with her in the first place. He needed a bit of a tete-a-tete with a rather scheming lady.

"I am glad to hear it," Rhett responded and would have made inquiries about their travel and other such useless pleasantries which were required by polite society had not a flutter of green fabric caught his eye.

"That is Miss Bingley." Mrs. Whimple's tone was cool.

"Yes, I know," Rhett replied. "Her brother-in-law is a friend of mine."

"So then, you know she is from trade?" There was no mistaking the derisiveness of the comment.

"Yes, I do," Rhett assured the lady. "And I hear her brother has virtually cut her off." He smiled at Mrs. Whimple's gasp. "It seems Mr. Bingley found a wife, and his sister did not approve of his choice. But then, Miss Bingley is a rather exacting female, is she not?"

"Oh, I should say so," said Miss Whimple. "She turns up her nose at so many gentlemen." The young lady made a small incredulous laughing sound. "As if one with family connections such as she has could be so choosy."

"Indeed," Rhett managed to reply politely.

He would rather have reminded the chit, whose nose was not precisely pointing downwards, that he himself had come into his current wealthy state due to relations in trade. However, he had other plans which would be aided by a shrewish gossip.

"I wonder if all the gents know of her familial connections or if they only know she is an heiress? She does have twenty thousand pounds, and that can be very persuasive to a man, unlike myself, who is perhaps a little short in the pockets."

"I am certain they could be made aware," said Mrs. Whimple, her delightfully pleasant smile running contrary to the calculating suggestion of her comment.

"It would perhaps save a fellow or two from falling into the wrong situation, do you not think?" Rhett returned her smile as he asked the question. Indeed, he did wish to ensure that Caroline did not fall into any situation with any other fellow but not for the reason Miss Whimple or her aunt was likely thinking. "It might even be worth a walk around the garden after dinner has concluded. I have it on good authority from Mr. Hadaway that such a thing may indeed be possible this evening before the instrument is opened and the music begins."

Mrs. Whimple's brow rose. "I shall see it done, and you may claim Charlotte for a stroll."

Rhett gave her a slight bow and his thanks before crossing the room to greet Hurst.

Chapter 3

"Twenty thousand," Mr. Thomas whispered to Mr. Stark. "However, there is not a drop of gentleman's blood in her veins, and," he lowered his voice even further, "I hear she is a bit of a harridan. Her brother has cut her off because she was so disagreeable about his choice of bride." Mr. Thomas shook his head. "Tis a pity what with her twenty thousand and her figure."

Rhett smiled and drained the last of the port from his glass. Mrs. Whimple had wasted no time in spreading the news of Caroline to her niece's dinner companion.

"Is that true, Hurst? Has Bingley cut her off?" Mr. Stark, who was not a softest-spoken man at the best of times and an even less soft spoken man at times such as this when he had consumed more port than he likely should have, called across the table to where Hurst sat next to Rhett.

"Aye," Hurst replied. "Foisted her off on me, so if anyone is looking for twenty thousand pounds, it is yours for the asking and the sooner, the better. I do not relish having to put up with her theatrics. I'll even toss in an extra five thousand if you take her before the end of the party. Compromise her. Steal her away to Gretna Green. It matters not to me how it is done, just that it is."

Rhett's brows rose. He knew that Hurst had agreed to play the part of displeased guardian of a troublesome sister, but it did seem he was going a wee bit over the top with his acting. Well, Rhett thought as he refilled his glass, perhaps it was not all acting. He knew Hurst did not get on well with his wife's younger sister because Caroline held far too much confidence in herself and bent Louisa to her will on a regular basis — even if that will was against Hurst's desires. However, in Rhett's opinion, if either Bingley or Hurst had bothered to check the girl before now, perhaps she would not need the lesson he was attempting to teach her. She would be the proper chit she was supposed to be instead of the troublesome, egotistical lady she was.

He swirled his drink as the conversation about the ladies in attendance swirled about the room. Caroline had not always been as she was now. He had met her first, many years ago when she was just a child, and he not yet a man. It had been shortly after her mother had died if he remembered correctly.

She had arrived in Manchester to stay with her aunt, and he had been accompanying his father on a business matter. She had smiled at him and thanked him when he held the door for her as she entered the shop. And he had, much to his father's displeasure, paid more attention to the young fairy-like girl with the copper curls and large brown eyes who was engaging a shop girl in a conversation than he had to what his father wished him to learn. He did not remember what Caroline had been speaking to the shop girl about, nor did it matter.

It was the way Caroline had treated the girl, for Caroline had not approached her as if the girl was a servant but as if she were deserving of respect. He had never forgotten that image. It was what he wished for in a wife. He had known it to some extent then and even more fully now. Caroline's nature was not that of a harridan. He took a sip of his drink. Not at her core anyway. The molding of that respectful, pleasant child into the woman Caroline now was the result of her aunt's training no doubt, for Caroline's aunt was not well-known in Manchester for her charity but rather her lack of that particular quality.

"Would it be an easy feat to compromise her, Hurst?"

Rhett rolled his eyes. Stark was still at it. Did the man have any idea of what proper decorum was?

Hurst shrugged. "She has been tossing herself at Darcy for two years. If your coffers are full, and your estate is half what Darcy's is, it should not be too difficult."

Rhett kicked Hurst's leg lightly under the table and raised a brow at him. Did he really wish for someone like Stark attempting to compromise Caroline? The man was known to be low on funds, and any money that would come to him would be mismanaged. To Rhett, there was no greater sign of weak character than a man who mismanaged his funds.

"All will be well," Hurst whispered, leaning toward Rhett. "She would not allow so much as a kiss unless an estate is three-quarters what Pemberley is." He smirked. "Besides, we did wish to give her a taste of what she has done to others, did we not?"

Rhett sighed and nodded. "She already threw herself into my arms this afternoon." He smiled as Hurst sputtered on his drink. "Her attitude may be frosty, but her body is not," he added with a lifted brow and a wicked grin.

Hurst was looking at him with wide eyes.

Rhett shrugged in response. "All will be well, will it not?" he asked softly before raising his voice again and adding. "I would marry her myself as I am always looking to increase my coffers," he picked a piece of lint from his sleeve, "not that my coffers are not already full." He smiled and took a sip of his beverage. "However, I do not have an estate," he sighed. "So, I shall just have to sample the wares and not purchase."

"You will both purchase a wife and an estate if you are going to sample Caroline's wares," Hurst muttered.

Again, Rhett shrugged. "If you have a lead on an

estate, then I might be willing to arrange a compromise unless one of you other gents would prefer to fill the role? We could play for the chance or some such thing."

Hurst shook his head and began to lift his glass to his lips. However, the glass never reached his mouth for it stopped in mid air as his mouth dropped open and then slid into a pleased smile. He knew precisely the estate Rhett should purchase for it would take care of two issues in one fell swoop. Bingley would be released from his lease, and Caroline would, for years to come, feel a portion of the discomfort she had caused for himself and Bingley. He lowered his glass and tipped his head as he looked at Rhett. "I know just the place."

~*~*~

Two and a half hours later, as the end of the intermission between musical performances was ending, Caroline returned to her seat next to Louisa and Hurst. The chair next to her was vacant. Mr. Pritchard had occupied it for the first half of the performances, but just moments ago, after having visited the refreshment table in the dining room, Mr. Pritchard had returned and made his excuses. There was a matter to which he needed to attend and would likely not be returned before the beginning of the first song, and since it would be rude to distract one and all with a late arrival, he would stand at the back once he rejoined the festivities. All this Caroline explained in hushed tones to her sister.

"That is most odd," said Louisa. "He has yet to quit the room."

Indeed, Mr. Pritchard was smiling and nodding at something Miss Wallace was saying and did not look as if he were in any hurry to end the conversation.

Caroline shrugged. "I cannot understand it." In her mind, she went over her interactions with the gentleman. There was nothing that she had done or said that should have been off-putting. She watched as Mr. Pritchard took a seat next to Miss Wallace, and Miss Wallace, seeing Caroline watching, raised a brow and smiled at her.

"You are certain this estate is not worth the pain of a trying mother?" Caroline asked her sister with a sad smile.

Louisa patted her hand. "All will be well. I will not have you here. It simply would not do."

Caroline allowed the matter to drop and prepared to listen to the upcoming performances.

"I can understand it," Miss Whimple said in a carrying whisper to Miss Blevins. "One does not rise from the mire of trade in one jump. Her goals are far too lofty for one of her station. Did you ever see the way she threw herself into the path of Mr. Darcy." Miss Whimple tittered as Caroline gasped. "Despicable. As if she had a chance of securing such a man. So grasping."

Caroline's eyes narrowed, and she turned to face her attacker despite Louisa's attempts to keep her from doing so. "I have far more to offer a gentleman than you," she snapped. "You have what? Three thousand pounds and," she let her eyes sweep up and down Miss Whimple, "a plump figure that shall only grow fatter with childbearing?"

Miss Whimple's face grew red. "My father has an estate."

Caroline shrugged. "For now, until the creditors will no longer extend him grace. Do not think that I have not heard of his unfortunate propensities to gamble and keep a stable of mistresses. However, since you do take after your mother in looks, I find I cannot entirely fault him for his pastimes. It will likely be the same with whomever you finally snare."

Miss Whimple sputtered and was clearly unable to speak a word in her own defense, but Miss Blevins' tongue was not tied, and so she rose to the defense of her friend. "At least, her husband will know he is marrying a maiden. The same cannot be said about you." She turned to her friend. "Did you hear that Miss Bingley threw herself into the arms of a gentleman already. I dare say her skirts are not heavy." She shot a smug grin at Caroline. "But what do you expect from one of her lot?"

"I did no such thing!" Caroline declared.

"I beg your pardon," said Rhett. "Is this seat taken?" He had stood just a short distance away and listened to the full conversation. It seemed Stark, who had walked out in the garden with Miss Blevins, had done his job quite proficiently.

"Mr. Rhett," Miss Whimple smiled sweetly at him. "There is room here. Miss Blevins can move over, and you can sit between us."

"A lovely offer, I am sure," he replied with a smile. "However, I should like to sit here with Miss Bingley if she will allow it. Hurst," he called down the row, "since Pritchard is otherwise entertained, you do not mind if I sit with your sister, do you?"

Caroline's mouth dropped open. He did not need Hurst's permission, nor did he need to ask it in such a loud voice as if he was attempting to draw attention to himself and the fact that her partner had left her.

"No, no," Hurst assured him. "I do not mind in the least."

"Good." Rhett unbuttoned his jacket and took a seat next to Caroline.

"She is beneath him," Miss Blevins whispered to Miss Whimple.

Rhett turned his head in Miss Blevins' direction. "Not yet," he whispered with a wink, "but the night is young."

He nearly laughed at the look of shock on the faces of the ladies behind him, and the look of horror on Miss Bingley's face required a firm bite to his cheeks to keep from snorting. If he were a betting man, which he was when the odds were in his favor, he would place ten pounds on the fact that his comment had earned him what he sought — a private audience with a lady whose prospects of making a good match were quickly dwindling to just one man — him.

Chapter 4

Caroline fidgeted with her fan and tapped her foot throughout the full half hour of performances. Then, when it was over, she rose quickly, gave a mumbled word of goodnight to Mr. Rhett, and pleaded with Louisa to see her to her room. She was not lying when she claimed a headache. Her head was throbbing, and her stomach was turning in unsettling twisting circles. The whispers had not stopped behind her. She had heard her name at least three times and several sniggers. And then, there was Mr. Rhett who kept smiling at her in the most teasing fashion as his knee often bumped hers and his hand brushed her thigh when he shifted position during Miss Morgan's dreadful rendition of some indecipherable song.

Louisa readily acquiesced to Caroline's pleas, but Hurst stood in their path.

"I believe a bit of fresh air would be just the thing," he said. "One short stroll in the garden, then, a bit of watered wine and bed. It will work like a charm. You will be feeling in fine fettle by the time the sun rises." He lifted a brow and gave Caroline a firm glare as she opened her mouth to protest.

Caroline clamped her lips closed and scowled.

"Rhett, you will join us, will you not?" Hurst continued.

Caroline shook her head slightly and formed the word no silently, but to no avail. Her brother was not to be moved from his position.

"I should like nothing better," Rhett replied. "It shall give me some time to get acquainted with Miss Bingley."

Caroline's eyes narrowed. She had no desire to spend another moment with a man who had implied that she was the sort of lady to be easily seduced, and she began to say as much until Hurst cleared his throat and gave her another stern look. She drew and released a slow breath.

"It would be my pleasure, Mr. Rhett," she said with a tight smile.

"Excellent," said Hurst. Taking his wife's hand

and placing it on his arm, he moved out of the row of chairs and began making his way to the garden just as several other couples and chaperones were doing.

"You have had a full card of gentlemen attending you this evening," Rhett began. "First Mr. Hadaway at dinner — now that is an honor to be seated with your host on first arrival. Then Mr. Thompson to escort you about the garden — he is a fine catch, I hear. And half a concert with Mr. Pritchard — lovely estate he has. And then me — my fortune is large, and I am a handsome devil."

Caroline's mouth dropped open and then snapped shut. Such arrogance!

"And it seems you are pretty and rich enough for the other ladies to already be attempting to throw you over," he continued. He watched her hand come up to her lips, and her finger began a tapping pattern. "I dare say I do not know why Mr. Pritchard would leave you for that Miss Wallace with the ears that stick out." He shook his head when she looked up at him in shock. "They make her look like a mouse."

"You are very rude, sir."

"Am I? Is this not how the matchmaking game

is played in polite society?" His voice dripped with disdain. "Do not we go about telling stories and pointing out the conquests, as well as the faults of others? I had thought you would be aware of this. You always seem to have some bit of something to whisper to your sister or a friend when at the soirees in town."

Caroline's brows furrowed. "How do you know what I do in town?"

He shrugged. "I watch people. There are those matrons who will welcome me due to my wealth and will allow me to dance with their charges, but then there are those, such as yourself, who lift their noses and walk the opposite direction because my money does not come from the possession of land."

Caroline sucked in a breath. Mr. Pritchard had been speaking to Mr. Rhett just before exiting the refreshments room. She had seen them in earnest conversation.

"You told him something to make him not like me," she accused.

"I am sorry. I do not follow." He was confident he knew what she was muttering about, but it was always best to get clarification before coming to a definite conclusion. He led her off the main path and down toward a small pavilion in a more secluded section of the garden.

"Mr. Pritchard. You were speaking with him while he was getting some lemonade. You wished him to ignore me as I had ignored you."

Rhett shrugged once again. There was some truth in what she was saying. He did wish for her to feel the treatment she had given to many over the last two years.

"Perhaps I did, or perhaps, I just wanted to have you for myself. And, seeing that I have no estate just yet, I thought it necessary to dissuade the competition."

Caroline attempted to pull her hand away from his arm, but he covered it with his free hand and held it firmly in place as he manoeuvred a very rattled Caroline up the two steps into the pavilion.

"I will have an estate," he said as he pulled her along. "I have just tonight learned of a prime opportunity, and should I be fortunate enough to find a wife among the ladies gathered here at Burton Hall, I shall not waste a minute in securing it. Indeed, I shall send my intent tomorrow."

"You are buying an estate?" Caroline realized

they had stopped walking and looked about. "Where are we? Where is Hurst?"

"We are in the garden, and I am fairly certain, Hurst is also somewhere in the garden. He is a man of his word, you know, and he did say he was going to take a walk in the garden." Rhett faced her, and as he expected, Caroline took a step backward. "Do not worry about Hurst. I have his full approbation." He stepped closer to her and ran his right hand up her right arm. "I think we would suit very well."

"You cannot know that," Caroline said, stepping backward again and bumping into a column of stone.

"I can," he said. "I am very good at deciphering things and am an excellent judge of character most times. In fact, there have been so few times I have been incorrect about a person that you would only need one set of fingers to count them." He ran his left hand up her left arm so that soon he had both her shoulders in his grip.

"We have only just met." Caroline attempted to shrug out of his grasp, although even to herself she had to admit it was a weak attempt. There was something very compelling about his eyes and his touch.

He shook his head and chuckled. "No, we met years ago, and I have seen you several times since. And then, I have heard about you from both your sister and Hurst."

"But we have never spoken."

"We are speaking now, are we not?"

"No, not exactly. You are holding me in place and telling me things, but that is not speaking. Perhaps after a half-hour of canvassing various topics, you will find me dull, and I will find you a bore. And then neither of us will wish to ever speak to the other again." Her tongue darted out to wet her lips. The way his thumbs were brushing back and forth on her shoulders where he held her was sending delightful little shivers down her spine.

He chuckled and released his hold on her. "I am never a bore," he said as he moved across the small pavilion to lean against the pillar opposite her. "And I rarely change my mind once I have made it."

"You seem very sure of yourself."

He inclined his head in acceptance. "I am, but not without just cause." He tipped his head. "First topic. The weather. I prefer sunshine or a light shower to fog and you?"

"Fog is rather dreary, and rain is a bother, so sunshine is my favourite weather," Caroline replied.

He smiled. "I thought so."

"You did not," she protested. "You are just saying that now that you know my answer."

"No," he shook his head. "You prize your appearance and neither rain nor fog aides a lady in presenting herself to best advantage."

"A fortunate guess."

"Town or country?" he asked, ignoring her rebuttal.

Caroline lifted a brow. "You tell me. Which do I prefer, Mr. Rhett?"

He shrugged. "That is easy. Town. For you do sparkle at a soiree. However, as the mistress of your own estate with the means to host dinners and balls, you would soon learn to enjoy the country nearly as much as town, though not entirely as much since there is less chance of a crush in the country and every good hostess lusts after a crush. It is the making of her, they say." He shrugged. "I prefer the town but am not opposed to taking an estate within a day's drive of London. Country air can be refreshing, and a good hunt is not to be missed."

Caroline snapped her lips closed. His reply was accurate. She smiled. "Happiness in marriage," she said, supplying the next topic of discourse. "Can it be predicted?"

"Do you wish for me to answer for myself or for you?"

Her brows furrowed as she considered his question. She would like to know his thoughts on the matter, but she also wondered if he truly knew her own.

"Both," she finally replied.

"Well," he said, pushing off the column and approaching her, "I think it can be predicted. Watch how a couple interacts in a ballroom. Is she aloof, and he distracted? Their life will not be a happy one. She will spend all of his money attempting to fill the void she feels at his absence, for he will spend a great amount of time at his clubs and with his mistress. However, if a gentleman is attentive to a lady, and she does not shy away from his touch and blushes at his compliments, they will likely be satisfied with one another and be quite happy." He leaned against the side of the column and, taking hold of her hand, held it as he continued. "You, on the other hand, think it is merely a coincidence that two people fall into a happily married state, for you do not seek the proper qualifications in a marriage partner."

She tried to pull her hand away from him, but he would not relinquish it. "I know precisely what qualifications are required for an advantageous marriage."

He lifted her fingers to his lips and kissed them softly. "Advantageous is not the same as good." He kissed her fingers again. "Character is more important than money, for a weak character will either waste his money or cling to it so tightly that he will never get any enjoyment from it."

He smiled at her. "You know this, and it is part of the reason you set your cap at Darcy. He is not only a man of wealth but a man of good character." He was enjoying the feel of her hand in his as well as the fact that she was not protesting when he pressed his lips against it once again.

"Gossip," he said as he leaned his head back on the column and gazed out into the cloudless, star-filled sky. "Is it just part of how one must function in society or is it a tool to use to get what you desire or exact revenge?"

"I...I...I believe it is just part of society," she stammered.

"It is unavoidable then?" he asked, turning for just a moment to look at her before once again gazing out into the near blackness."I believe it should be avoided most times," he continued as he rubbed the back of her hand with his thumb.

She sighed. His thumbs were certainly adept at making her feel quite wonderful.

"Did you enjoy the tales Miss Whimple was telling?" He heard her quick intake of breath at his question. "I thought not, and I dare say, if I were to go back to the house and over a game of billiards share with Mr. Stark how we were alone in this pavilion, you would also not appreciate that, would you?"

"You would do no such thing! Would you?"

He shrugged. "I might."

"But you said you thought gossip should be avoided," she argued.

"Most times," he retorted. "However, there are times when gossip would work in one's favor, such as, say if one wished to make all other gentlemen shun a lady so that she has no option but to choose him since she only has until next Saturday to secure an offer."

Caroline gave her hand a firm tug and extracted it from his grip. "That is vicious."

He turned and leaned sideways on the column so he could see her. "Is it any less barbarous than what you have done to your brother, as well as Miss Bennet and her sister?" He smiled as her eyes grew wide. "Hurst told me."

She scowled and crossed her arms.

"It is not who you are." He shrugged. "That is why you will find that there may be other gentlemen here who will think you welcoming of a bit of a seduction, but they will not be offering for you."

"What did you do?" She was finding it hard to breathe. "I will be sent to my aunts for good if I do not find a husband."

He sighed. "I have only done to you what you have done to others. I may have mentioned your roots are in trade — which we know should be below a gentleman's acceptance." He shrugged. "But Stark would likely overlook such a thing since his estate is in need of propping up and your twenty thousand would do well for him. So, that is why I might have exaggerated our little collision outside the library earlier and made the comment I did to Miss Blevins. Your reputation is, well," he smiled and pushed off the column, "precarious." He stepped in front of her so closely that she could feel his warmth reaching out to her. "How does it feel to be treated so?"

She blinked as tears gathered.

His hands found their way back to her shoulders. "This is how you have made others feel, and I can see from the tears in your eyes that you are not lost to all good sense. That girl who smiled at a manufacturer's son and talked with respect to a shop-girl is still in you."

She shook her head.

"Yes," he said, leaning closer, "she is there, and I am rarely wrong about these things." His lips brushed hers, faintly, softly, like a whisper of the wind that flutters a curtain on a warm summer day. And then, summoning a great deal of fortitude, he moved away.

"My offer has already been accepted by Hurst. I have only to ask for your acceptance. Do you think we will suit?" He placed a finger on her lips to keep her from replying. "It matters not, for I know we shall. And I am rarely wrong, and I am even less likely to change my mind."

He stood back and offered her his arm. "I will ask you properly in three day's time. That should be long enough for you to know that I am indeed correct."

"You are very sure of yourself, " she finally said. They had made it nearly from the pavilion and back to the path before she found her voice as her senses had been thoroughly overwhelmed first by his closeness, then by his light kiss, and finally by his finger on her lips and the intense look in his eyes as he spoke.

He lifted her fingers to his lips once again, and after kissing them, replied, "I am, but not without just cause." He smiled at her look of consternation and then led her back along the path toward the house.

Chapter 5

"Mr. Rhett has been at your side at every turn," Louisa said two days later as she climbed on the bed to sit next to Caroline. "And tomorrow is the third day since his overtures in the garden." She placed a pillow between her back and the bedpost so that she could rest against it with more comfort. "Will you accept his offer?"

Caroline had, of course, been required to tell her sister all that had happened in the garden. "If he is going to purchase an estate in a timely manner, then yes, I believe I will accept."

Louisa hugged her knees tightly and squealed softly. It was late, or perhaps she might have been more vocal in her delight. "Hurst assures me that he is indeed purchasing an estate. Letters have been sent, and the agreement should not be far off."

"That is what Mr. Rhett has told me as well," said Caroline. "He seems to understand the importance of such things. It is a good quality to find in a gentleman."

"Do you like or, perhaps, love him?" Louisa tipped her head and studied her sister's face.

Caroline fidgeted. She had been considering that very fact. She knew in reality that she had no options open to her since the other gentlemen in attendance had shown her very little attention, and what attention they had shown had either been a haughty demeanor or a winking eye with a wish to find a secluded corner.

"It matters not," Caroline replied. "I must have a husband by the end of this party, and I do not see another stepping forward."

Louisa gasped, and her mouth dropped open. "But would you wish for another to step forward. Has not Mr. Rhett been kind and attentive? Has he not shown you respect and stared down at least two men who have spoken to you meanly?"

Caroline would have liked to have forgotten about the comments Mr. Pritchard and Mr. Thompson had made about her. She neither liked being referred to as a shrew or a pleasant way to warm your bed. She was not intended to hear the comments, but she had, and Rhett had been at her side and heard them as well.

"I thought it very likely that he was going to call one or the other out, and, I can tell you," Louisa leaned forward and whispered, "for I have sneaked a peek at the men while they are training in the morning, that I do not think any man would stand a chance against Mr. Rhett. He is very adept with a sword."

Caroline smiled. Her sister was not the only one who had dared to catch a glimpse of the gentleman as they sparred. Rhett did cut a fine figure. "While I can admire his swordsmanship, it does not necessitate that I love or even like him." Did it? She had spent an inordinate amount of time thinking about him and writing the letter *R* in her notebook.

"Do you not think you would suit?" Louisa asked.

"Whether one suits or does not suit does not indicate love either," Caroline retorted and then sighed. "I like him very much, I suppose. We have not lacked topics of conversation, and I have enjoyed talking with him, even if he is always telling me what I think."

And he was so often right. It was as if he understood everything about her. The thought had been unsettling at first, but now, it was beginning to feel rather comforting. No other person had ever understood her desire for acceptance. Why else had she listened so closely to what her aunt said? Why else had she behaved just as her friends at school told her she should? Why else did she lash out when she felt she was being forced away or left behind? It was because she craved acceptance.

"He is handsome," she continued, "and financially sound, and soon, he shall be in possession of an estate. His taste in music mirrors my own, and though he does not find art to be of great interest, he has a discriminating eye. I should think he would allow me to decorate a home as I saw fit without imposing anything garish or gauche. Every jacket he has worn has been of fine quality, and his manners while eating are not disturbing like Mr. Stark's."

Louisa giggled. "I do not know why Mr. Stark thinks we all wish to see the contents of his mouth as he eats."

"Nor do I," Caroline responded with a light laugh. "Do you think Mr. Rhett and I are a good match?" A flutter of nerves danced in her chest and caused her head to feel slightly light as she waited for her sister's response. It seemed very important for some reason that Louisa approved of Mr. Rhett. Caroline already knew that Hurst approved, but he would have approved of any gentleman who had offered just to be rid of her. He had not been backward in letting her know such was true.

There was a tap at the door, and Louisa climbed off of the bed and scurried across the room to answer it. "I do. I truly do," she said before she pulled the door open.

"Mrs. Hurst," said Rhett with a smile. "Your husband instructed me to relay a message to you since I would be passing Miss Bingley's room on the way to mine. He said to inform you that he has played his last hand and wishes to retire."

"Oh, very good. I thank you and shall go to him directly in a moment." She smiled. "Have a pleasant night, Mr. Rhett."

"Goodnight to you as well, my dear," he said with a wink, causing her to giggle as she closed the door.

"I must go to Hurst, but I also do wish you to know how exceedingly happy I am for you, Caroline." She bent and gave her sister a kiss on the forehead. "I shall see you in the morning so that I can help you pick the gown that will make Mr. Rhett the happiest of men to be accepted by such a woman as you." She tucked the blankets around Caroline, and with one last soft kiss to her sister's forehead, considered her duties done for the night and left to go to her own room.

~*~*~

Caroline followed her sister from the breakfast room to the garden. The sun was shining brightly, and there was a dry, gentle breeze fluttering the petals of the flowers and rustling the leaves of the trees. The ladies of the party were gathered on a knoll with their chaperones not far away, keeping an eye on the gentlemen as they wandered through the garden and made their way to where their charges sat. Caroline stood at the bottom of the knoll, wishing she did not have to go sit with the other ladies, but Louisa had thought it best. Mr. Rhett would surely look for her there, Louisa has assured her.

He had not been in the breakfast room that morning, and she had not seen him return with the men who had been out riding, and now as she took a tentative seat on the edge of the group of young ladies, she did not see him with the other gentlemen.

She plucked a blade of grass and wound it around her finger and then unwound it as she glanced expectantly back at the house. Perhaps Mr. Rhett was talking with Hurst. He seemed to enjoy spending time with her sister's husband. It was a good thing, she supposed, since that would guarantee her frequent visits from Louisa. Her heart pinched. She would miss Charles as he would likely never darken her door. She sighed and plucked another blade of grass. That is, he would likely never darken her door unless she apologized. But how could she? It would be entirely too humiliating to have to lower oneself to beg forgiveness from Charles's wife and Mrs. Darcy.

"Miss Bingley, you are looking thoughtful," said Mr. Stark, "and that shade of yellow does you justice like no other shade might."

Caroline lifted a brow at his obvious flattery. "Thank you," she said.

"I am promised to Miss Blevins for a stroll through the roses, but perhaps later, we might have our turn and a private conversation."

Caroline's brows furrowed at the emphasis he put on the words private conversation. "A stroll would be lovely, but it must be had in public with my sister in attendance."

"I assure you, Miss Bingley, there is nothing untoward in my suggestion, and I have your brother's approbation to speak to you in private."

"You have what?" Caroline's heart leapt to her throat. Had Hurst not given Mr. Rhett his acceptance? Why was Mr. Stark now speaking as if he had it? She looked around, desperately hoping to see Mr. Rhett somewhere in the garden or exiting the house.

"He is not here," Mr. Stark said.

"Who is not here?" Caroline asked.

"Mr. Rhett. That is for whom you were looking, is it not?"

The reply stole the air from Caroline's lungs for a moment. He was gone? But today was the day he was to offer for her.

"He had some business which needed attending," Mr. Stark explained and then smiled and bowed as Miss Blevins, with parasol twirling, joined him.

"Who is attending to business when there is

such a fine garden in which to stroll?" Miss Blevins batted her lashes and gave Caroline a feigned friendly smile.

"Mr. Rhett," Mr. Stark replied before Caroline could do more than open her mouth. "He was all in a bluster about something this morning. It seemed as if he could not get his carriage ready fast enough for his tastes. But then, he does rather seem the doing sort of fellow. So I imagine it is not a thing to worry about too terribly much. It is likely nothing of grave importance, just a desire to be done doing what needs to be done."

"Indeed," said Miss Blevins with a smirk.

"Oh, there is Mr. Thompson," Mr. Stark waved to the gentleman as he approached the group of ladies. "I had a thing to tell him. You do not mind waiting a moment while I do so, do you, Miss Blevins?"

"No, I shall keep Miss Bingley company until you return." She waited quietly until Mr. Stark was well away from them. Then, she turned to Miss Bingley. "It appears Mr. Rhett got what he desired, so he left."

Caroline blinked. "Pardon me? I do not comprehend your meaning."

Miss Blevins pursed her lips. "I saw him telling you goodnight at your door last night."

"He did no such thing!" Caroline cried.

Miss Blevins shrugged. "I can only say what I heard and saw, and I saw him outside your door, wishing you a good night." She shook her head. "One must learn to be more discreet when carrying out an assignation."

Caroline could not believe what she was hearing. "I assure you, he only stopped to tell my sister that her husband was finished playing cards. I did not even speak to him."

Miss Blevins lifted a brow and shrugged as Mr. Stark returned. "That may be your story, but it is not the one everyone else has heard. I do believe you are done both here and in town." She spun and greeted Mr. Stark, and then with a self-satisfied grin to Caroline, accepted Mr. Stark's arm and meandered away.

Caroline huffed at the back of Miss Blevins' departing figure. "She is horrid," she said as she rose to her feet. "She and her simpering and smirking and batting of her lashes — ghastly, simply ghastly! How anyone could behave in such a fashion is beyond my comprehension," Caroline muttered as she made her way to where her sister sat. "Louisa, I must speak with you."

"She is a demanding sort, is she not?" Caroline heard Mrs. Carlyle say and turned toward her with a glare.

"And your charge is an ill-mannered, story-weaving, ogress!" Caroline flicked her head and marched toward the house with Louisa scampering after her.

She did not stop until she had reached the hall outside the library. She paced back and forth in front of the library door, one hand resting at the base of her throat, and the other firmly placed on her hip.

"Whatever has happened, Caroline." Louisa paced behind her sister.

"He is gone. Gone." Caroline shook her head.

"Who is gone?"

"And without a word to me," Caroline continued not even hearing her sister's question. "He was supposed to offer for me today. He said he would. He made me believe he intended to marry me." She turned to her sister. "How could he do that?"

"Ah, Caroline, Louisa, I was just coming to find the two of you." Hurst stood at the library door.

"Come in." He made a sweeping motion with his hand. "I have some good news, I think." He tipped his head and looked at Caroline, who was still pacing in the hall. "Is she well?" he asked his wife.

Louisa shook her head and, taking Caroline by the arm, guided her into the library. "I believe Mr. Rhett has defected."

"And this has her dismayed?" Hurst schooled his features to look concerned while inwardly he smiled. It was good to see Caroline so affected by a man. He had never thought she would be. Indeed, he had oft wondered if she even possessed a heart.

Louisa nodded. "He was to offer today," she whispered.

"Yes, well, there is no need to be disheartened. I have a second option for you, Caroline. He is not as well off financially, but his estate has been in his family for several generations and when his uncle dies, which is expected to happen in the next year or so — his uncle is not a healthy or young man, you see — this gentleman will come into a great deal of money and land. And we both know that is something for which you have always wished."

Caroline stopped pacing and looked at Hurst with her mouth hanging open. He could not be speaking of Mr. Stark. She shook her head. No matter the size of that man's estate or the number of pounds in his bank account, she would not accept him.

"He is no Mr. Darcy to be sure," Hurst continued, "but he is not repulsive. Many of the other ladies seem to have set their caps at him. Miss Blevins has certainly made a point of following him about." Hurst chuckled at the look of horror on Caroline's face. Apparently, she had figured out of whom he was speaking.

"I know how you would enjoy besting that pretentious miss. You would be the envy of many once he comes into his full inheritance. Pin money, carriages, gowns, balls — you will have it all and be a gentleman's wife, which brings with it that status you have always craved. He is not opposed to a tradesman's daughter, so I expect he will treat you well."

Caroline shook her head. "No. No."

"You do not wish to be a gentleman's wife?"

Caroline slumped into a chair. "I do not want *him*. You will have to send me to my aunt." Tears hung perilously close to falling.

Hurst sat down across from her. "You would

choose to live in Manchester instead of marrying Mr. Stark?"

Caroline's lip quivered as she nodded her head. "I cannot marry him."

"Why?" Hurst prodded gently.

"I do not care for him. He does not close his mouth when he chews, and he likes to talk of nothing but himself and the latest gossip. He is quite distasteful." And he was not Mr. Rhett. There was no one, her heart cried, who could stand in the place of Mr. Rhett. "I would rather not marry."

Hurst's brows rose. "Stark will be disappointed. I had given him permission to seek you out."

She nodded. "I know. He mentioned it when I saw him in the garden."

Hurst leaned back and studied his sister. There was a decided change in her. He had not thought Rhett capable of affecting a change in Caroline, and he certainly had not expected it to happen so quickly. "Very well, I shall speak to Stark."

"Thank you." Caroline rose to leave. "I do not feel well. I shall retire to my room for the remainder of the day." She paused. "Do you know why Mr. Rhett left?"

"I could not say," Hurst replied, although he had

a very good idea as to why Rhett was gone. "Men are fickle."

Caroline nodded. "Would you be terribly distressed if I asked to leave tomorrow?"

"You wish to leave?" Louisa said in shock.

"I have no prospects here, and the things they are saying about me are absolutely horrid."

"What are they saying?" Hurst prodded.

"Someone saw Mr. Rhett saying goodnight to Louisa at my door last night and assumed he had been in my room visiting me." Her cheeks flushed a brilliant red and tears once again threatened. She swallowed. "They said he got what he wanted and that is why he left."

Hurst turned to his wife. "See that all is made ready. We will leave in the morning."

Chapter 6

Caroline looked back at Burton Hall as Hurst's carriage turned from the drive onto the main road. It was a grand estate. The windows marched in two smart lines across its facade, and hedges stood in fine array protecting the garden at its side. Through the gate and down the path, she knew there were a fountain and circular walk with benches around it, flanked by carefully tended flowers.

She rested her head against the side of the window. To look at it, Burton Hall was perfect — everything she would have dreamt of managing as an estate's mistress. The gardens would flourish. The house would be filled on a regular basis with friends and family. Chatter would surround the dining table and waft down the halls from the drawing room. And she had thought that those things were the only things that were needed to have a fulfilling life, but now, remembering how empty that great house with all its guests had felt, her heart ached, and she knew there was something more that was necessary to her happiness.

She wished for someone with whom to share it. Not an acquaintance or a guardian — someone who was more, someone who understood her and talked to her and accepted her faults while assuring her they could be improved. She longed for someone like Mr. Rhett.

She sighed again. No, not someone like him — him. He was, she realized, quite likely the one man in the whole of the British Empire who in disposition was best suited to her. She peeked back once again. The house could just be glimpsed before they descended a small rise.

"Do you suppose," she began, looking at Louisa, "that Charles felt this awful constricting in his chest when he was persuaded not to return to Netherfield?"

"I have not considered it," replied Louisa.

"He intended to marry Miss Bennet. We both knew he did."

Louisa nodded. "But you were certain it was not

a good match, and I could not see an error in your argument. Miss Bennet was lovely, but she was no more lovely to him than to the footmen."

Caroline shrugged. "I suppose it did not matter how Miss Bennet acted. We should have considered Charles's heart."

Louisa looked perplexed. "We did, did we not? You said he would be grievously injured by her refusal."

"If she had refused." Caroline smiled sheepishly and sneaked a peek at Hurst, whose lips were pursed in an attempt not to smirk. "I knew she preferred him."

Hurst chuckled softly as his wife gasped. Louisa truly was too easily led at times.

"I had thought that very thing, and yet, you denied it so vigorously that I thought I must be mistaken." Caroline's older sister's brows furrowed. "Although, I do not know why I figured I was wrong. I have never been wrong about such a thing in my life until then." She sat forward and held up a finger. "And apparently, I was not incorrect then either, so it remains that I have never been mistaken." She leaned back, satisfied with herself.

"Do you not wish to know why Caroline persuaded you that you were wrong?" her husband asked.

"Oh, I do not need to inquire," Louisa replied. "Caroline wished to marry Mr. Darcy, and Mr. Darcy would not return to Netherfield if Charles did not."

Hurst raised a brow and watched his wife's pretty lips purse and her brows furrow again until understanding dawned, and her mouth popped open and then closed while a blush crept up her cheeks as she realized her foolishness in not being able to reason that out before now.

"It is likely how Darcy felt leaving Netherfield as well, though I think he was deceiving himself more than Charles as to the reason necessary for his departure," added Hurst.

Caroline shrugged and turned her eyes again to the road for a few moments. Suddenly, she sat forward and looked first one direction up the road they travelled and then down. "This is not the north road," she said, looking at Hurst.

"No, it is not," he replied from behind his paper. "You will come home to Maplewood with us."

"But my aunt –"

"Is a cantankerous old biddy who will undo in five minutes the improvements Rhett has wrought in you," muttered Hurst. "And frankly, I have no desire to visit her."

The old woman, who was not actually all that old in age but only so in attitude, was constantly questioning Hurst on his family and holdings. She wished to know the state of his accounts and how he spent his money as well as why he had not been successful in getting his wife with child. In her last letter to Louisa, she had gone so far as to recommend a physician in town, known to her own physician, who might be of some help in sorting out the issue.

Added to these charges, Hurst knew that Bingley held their aunt as the source of Caroline's miseducation, and Hurst had seen such a glimmer of hope of improvement over the last three days that he dared not chance having Caroline relapse into her former trying self.

"Louisa will plan a dinner. Word of your ordeal has likely not reached every hamlet just yet." He turned the page and snapped the paper into a more readable upright position.

"But you said I must choose from the men at the party or go to Manchester."

"I changed my mind, but if you continue to protest, I will gladly find a coach that is going that direction. However, do not expect me to join you."

"No, no, I am not protesting," Caroline hurried to assure him. "I was merely confused." She slipped into silent contemplation again until Louisa clucked her tongue drawing Caroline's attention.

"Imagine how Miss Bennet must have felt upon our departure and your letter." She shook her head and sighed. "And then after, we were so rude in calling on her. She must have been beside herself with sorrow if she truly loved Charles, which she apparently did."

Caroline felt the sting of her sister's words. It had been she, not Louisa, who had decided that they would both receive and return Miss Bennet's call in such a fashion.

It would not do, she had told Louisa, for them to inflate the girl's hopes regarding their brother. He could do better. He could find a wife that would care for him more. Miss Bennet would soon be a memory since Charles never seemed to fancy one over another for any length of time. And Mr. Darcy would not be subjected to such lowly connections.

Caroline leaned back in her seat. Oh, Louisa was not entirely without fault. She had participated with alacrity in disparaging Hertfordshire and the Bennets with very little prompting from Caroline. However, it still remained that Caroline was the instigator of such deplorable, harmful behaviour. She closed her eyes and allowed her heart to feel her own pain as she contemplated how much she had caused for her brother and Miss Bennet.

Hurst smiled secretly at the forlorn look on Caroline's face as she rested her head against the side of the carriage. He could tell that she was finally beginning to see her actions in a fresh new light, and his wife, well, the kind-hearted lady he knew she could be, would soon stand forward once again now that Caroline was likely to be acting differently.

~*~*~

For two days of travel and another four at Maplewood, Caroline pondered both her own previous actions and the events from the house party.

"Oh, I have been such a fool," she said, dropping onto a bench in the garden.

"About what?" a deep voice inquired, causing Caroline to squeal and jump. "My apologies. I have been told I am light on my feet and should rattle the plants when I walk so others know I am coming." Rhett sat down on the bench next to her.

"Mr. Rhett," Caroline's hand, which had flown to her startled heart at the sound of his voice, still lay above that rapidly beating organ, "you are here."

"Indeed, I am." He tipped his head and smiled. "I take it you did not expect to see me."

Caroline blinked. "Why should I have expected to see you? You left without so much as a word of parting."

He shrugged, his smile becoming somewhat sheepish. "I must apologize for that. I had written a note of explanation to Hurst but in my haste and hurry to be gone, bundled it up with my other papers and took it with me rather than leaving it behind."

Caroline's brows rose. "You expect me to believe that?"

"Whether you choose to believe it or not, it is the truth." He pulled a small folded sheet of paper from his pocket and handed it to her. "It asks Hurst to inform you that I would return and make my offer as intended but that I wished to have an estate before I did so." He lifted his left shoulder and let it drop. "I wished for you to know I was in earnest about my promise to take an estate."

Caroline flipped open the folded sheet of paper he had handed her. It said exactly what he said it would. "How do I know you did not write this today before you arrived?"

"You do not."

Caroline's brows furrowed. She had expected him to protest and try to reason her into believing he had written the note when he claimed he had. However, he was doing what he had always done since she had met him — unsettling her with his direct, self-assured replies. It was as if nothing disturbed him.

She lifted her chin. "I do not know why you came." She kept her tone curt and watched his face closely for any sign of disquiet. There was none.

"I wish to marry you, and it is preferred in modern society that an application is made to the lady rather than just carting her off to the nearest parson. So I came." His lips curled into a smirk. "However, if you prefer carting, I will oblige."

She tried to keep her eyes from showing her surprise at his comments, but she could not. She wanted to tell him that carting her off might be the only way to get her to marry him after he had left her to such gossip, but just before the words flew from her mouth, she thought better of it, since, in all likelihood, he might actually cart her off.

"You may apply, but I may not accept."

He reached over and pulled the ribbon of her bonnet. "It will be easier to kiss you without that on your head," he explained as he removed the bothersome article.

"Kiss me? I think not!" she said, attempting to snatch her bonnet back from him. On being unsuccessful in reclaiming her hat, she shot to her feet. She was not going to sit within kissing distance. "You left me."

"Yes, but I have already explained about the note. I have secured an estate, and it just awaits its mistress and the few new pieces of furniture that I have ordered to be completed." He placed the bonnet on the bench and rose to stand in front of her. Her arms were folded protectively across her middle, and her eyes accused him of hurting her.

"Do you know what they said when you left?"

He drew a deep breath. He had a pretty good idea what it might have been. "No, what did they say?"

"They said you had gotten what you wanted from me and that is why you left. They said you did not want me. You only wished to seduce me."

Tears had gathered in her accusing eyes, and it took a great deal of determination on Rhett's part not to just pull her into his arms and apologize for the pain he knew he had intentionally caused. "I thought they might," he said.

"You knew they would whisper such things about me and still you left?"

The horror of such a thing etched across her face was his undoing. As much as he knew he should remain strong and feign nonchalance, he could not. He took one large step towards her and wrapped her in his arms. "I am sorry," he whispered. "I needed to be certain that you understood how it felt to be treated so meanly."

She attempted to extract herself from his embrace.

"It is precisely what you did to your brother and the Miss Bennets, and it is beneath you to behave so. You are a far better woman than that."

"I am not." The tears she had been fighting for nearly a week finally would be held back no longer, and she allowed herself to be held firmly against his chest as she wept for the pain she had caused her brother as well as the Bennets and even Darcy. "I have been abominable."

"Yes, my darling, you have been," Rhett said as he rubbed her back and pressed kisses in her hair. "But you are better than Miss Blevins or Miss Whimple." He pulled back just enough to see her face. "That kind little girl is still inside you." He smiled. "I am rarely wrong about these things."

Despite her tears, she laughed. "I cannot see her."

He bent his head and kissed her lightly. "I can, and I would be most delighted if she would do me the honour of becoming my wife." He kissed her once again. "I love you, Caroline. For all my life, I have loved you. Please, marry me."

Her eyes overflowed once again as she happily nodded her consent, and he claimed her smiling lips, not in a light kiss as he had before but in a kiss that demanded she return his affection and give herself to him. And she did. She wound her arms around his neck and allowed her body to meld to his.

He was not what she had expected to want in a husband. She had wished for a man of position and wealth. She had wished for an estate and carriages. She had wished for others to look at her and be envious of her situation. She sighed as he deepened the kiss.

She knew that others would be envious of her, but not because her husband was rich — though he was — or because his estate was grand — which she hoped it was — but because she had a husband who loved her enough to teach her a lesson — which, she knew, was better than she deserved.

Epilogue

"A trip with nothing at which to look is very dull," Caroline protested for the fourth time about the windows being draped in Rhett's carriage. They had married the very day Rhett had arrived at Maplewood. Apparently, he was indeed prepared to cart her off to the nearest parson, or more precisely, to cart the nearest parson to Maplewood to perform the duty of marrying them. The dinner Louisa had planned, suddenly became an impromptu wedding celebration.

Caroline had protested not having a gown specifically for her wedding or the opportunity to have wedding clothes made before they married.

Rhett, then, just as now, merely smirked and replied, "Do you think I have not considered that?"

He was pleased with the progress Caroline had made in turning away from her selfish attitudes and actions, but he was no fool. Change took time, and if not tended to properly, the small improvements that had been made would be lost.

It would be some time before his wife would be allowed to make more than the smallest of decisions without his input. It was not that he enjoyed being authoritative, per se, but he knew Caroline had been given free rein for much too long, and he would be hanged if he was going to allow it to continue. So, a bit of discomfort now would set the course for a very happy and relaxed later.

When they had returned to town the day after their wedding, Caroline had found that her wedding clothes — her very beautiful wedding clothes — had been ordered. Before Rhett had left Burton Hall, he had learned the name of Caroline's modiste from Hurst. Then, while he was in town retrieving a special license, it was a simple matter to have a friend's wife assist him in ordering all that was deemed necessary.

Caroline and Rhett had remained in town after their arrival just long enough for the clothes to be completed and the few items Rhett had ordered for their new estate to be delivered and set in place.

Then, having had a letter from his housekeeper,

Mrs. Nicholls, that all was ready to receive a new mistress, he had instructed Caroline to make ready to leave in the morning.

Caroline sighed and leaned back. There was no point in arguing the issue. Her husband refused to argue.

The seat on which she sat was immensely comfortable. Rhett's taste in vehicles was as good as his taste in fashion. He liked to have the best — that was he liked to have the best as long as he could have the best at the best price. Caroline was learning quickly that her husband was very exacting about many things — never overbearing, but particular that business and household affairs be conducted properly. He checked on her progress with the books, he liked to see the menus before they were approved, and he preferred to keep to a schedule as closely as possible.

Caroline smiled as Rhett slipped an arm around her and tugged her close. She was also learning that her husband enjoyed being near her and touching her. And she adored the way the right side of his mouth would tip up, as it was now, whenever she was delighted by something that he had done for her.

If Rhett were completely honest, he would have to admit that along with knowing he needed to continue his re-education of his wife, he delighted in caring for her and watching her eyes light with surprise. He only hoped that those lovely eyes would light with delighted surprise when she saw her new home, though he suspected, they would not.

Caroline had attempted to ferret out of him the location of the estate as well as the name, its size, and how many staff it boasted. He had refused to tell her anything of use. Instead, he would only tell her that it was well named and within a short distance in some direction from town, it was not overly grand, but it was impressive, and that its staff was exactly what it should be.

His thumb stroked her arm where his hand lay draped over her shoulder. They were drawing near their destination, and he needed to begin preparing her for their arrival. "Do you trust me to do what is best for you — for us?"

Caroline turned her head, her eyes wide with concern. "Is it a dreadful place, and you have only said it was lovely to lure me away from town?"

He smiled and shook his head. "No, it is lovely,

though not as lovely as you." He winked and kissed her nose, causing her to giggle. "Do you trust me?"

Caroline bit her lip as she considered the question. He had shown her the error of her ways in a most effective, though excruciating, fashion. He had chosen clothes for her that were flattering and stylish. He had shown her the things he had ordered for their new home and his selections were almost exactly as she would have made. She trusted him to know what was best, yet there was trepidation about his methods.

"Is it another painful lesson that I must learn?"

He shrugged. "It is not precisely a lesson so much as a constant reminder." And it would likely prove painful, at least, at first.

The carriage had turned from the main road and so, leaning across his wife, he removed one of the window coverings so that she might see where she was. It would be best for her to fly into a fit here in the privacy of the coach rather than in front of the staff.

Caroline's mouth dropped open. "Netherfield?"

"It is lovely, is it not?" he asked hopefully.

Her shoulders drooped, and she shook her head. She would not have in a million lifetimes expected to be arriving in Hertfordshire as the mistress of Netherfield. In fact, she had rather hoped she would never have to visit Hertfordshire again.

Rhett watched her wilt. Why was it that lessons and improvements were so very hard to teach? Why could not the pain of the lesson reside solely with the party requiring the instruction? Why must it also prick at the heart of the teacher?

He pulled her back to his side. "I love you," he said as he wrapped her in his embrace, "and I could think of nowhere better for you to demonstrate to the world that you are better than the Miss Blevins and Miss Whimples of the ton."

And he was right, as he nearly always was. Caroline, after the initial shock of seeing her new home and the uncomfortable reintroductions to people both on staff and in the neighbourhood to whom she had not been kind, rose to the challenge he placed before her.

Within a fortnight, she had hosted a dinner for the Bennets, the Philips, and the Lucases. After which, knowing that at least one letter had been sent to Derbyshire singing his wife's praises, Rhett finally allowed her to write her letters of apology to those she had harmed.

Michaelmas came and went. Mr. and Mrs. Rhett attended the assembly in Meryton. The Bennets returned from Lydia's wedding with greetings from Caroline's friends and relatives in Derbyshire.

In November, Caroline, with Rhett's encouragement, threw open the doors of Netherfield and hosted what would become a yearly ball.

In December, Caroline and Rhett returned to town both to celebrate Christmas with Louisa and Hurst and to prepare for the season.

The Bingleys and Darcys accepted invitations to dinner twice during that season, and witnessed first-hand, and with great surprise, Caroline's transformation.

And, well before spring was pushing away the dreariness of winter, Caroline no longer required the strictures Rhett had placed upon her. Slowly and with a heart that both rejoiced in his wife's improvement and grieved the loss of providing such constant care, he lifted them only to find, to his delight, that his wife sought his advice and wished to tell him about her day.

It was after all these things, in the early hours of the morning after returning from a soiree, that the

Rhetts prepared for bed and began, as they always did, a discussion about the events of the evening.

"Did you see Miss Whimple?" Caroline asked as she settled into bed next to her husband. "She is still pursuing Mr. Hadaway."

Rhett chuckled. "As I hear it, Hadaway's mother does not approve of Miss Whimple's lack of fortune, and Hadaway is not one to disappoint his mama."

Caroline snuggled into his side. "Mrs. Stark is spending a good deal of time watching the dancing while her husband is constantly losing his money at the card tables."

Again, Rhett chuckled. "Yes, well, it does appear from the roundness of her belly that Mr. Stark got what he wanted from Miss Blevins before he found himself obliged to marry her."

Caroline swatted his leg. "Such talk, Mr. Rhett!" She giggled. "Do you know that he intended to offer for me at Hadaway's house party?" She propped up on her elbow and looked down at him. "The day you left, Mr. Stark had asked Hurst for permission to speak with me alone." Her brows furrowed. "You do not look surprised."

He smiled sheepishly. "I may have had something to do with that."

"You?"

He nodded and pulled her down to lay her head on his chest. "It was a calculated gamble, but one I felt fairly confident I would win. You see, I was to leave that note with Hurst, and Hurst was to allow Mr. Stark to offer for you since Stark would in the next year or so have exactly what you had always wished for in a husband — a grand estate and a fortune." He kissed the top of her head. "Not that he would have retained that fortune for any great length of time, as you can tell by how well he succeeds at the card tables — which is likely why he accepted my money to make an offer." He gave her head another kiss as his hand began slowly stroking up and down her arm.

Caroline gasped. "You paid him to offer for me?"

"Yes, because... "

"I know why." Caroline interrupted, and her husband replied with a smile and silence. Caroline had become familiar with her husband's methods of instruction and was certain she could guess his reason. "You wished for me to have to choose between a man who had wealth but did not yet have an estate and a man who had the things I had deemed necessary for a husband to possess. Is that correct?"

Rhett nodded. "You are correct, although you forgot to mention that the first gentleman's fortune came from trade and the second's family had been finding their wealth in the land for generations."

She pushed up so that she could look at him. "You could have been wrong. I was so distraught when you left. I thought I had no other prospects."

He brushed a wisp of hair from her cheek and tucked it behind her ear. "You would not choose him. He is coarse. He speaks too loudly and too much, not to mention his manners when eating are in need of refinement."

"You are very certain of yourself, are you not?" She accused with a smile.

Rhett shrugged. "I am, but not without just cause." He lifted off his pillow and kissed her before flopping back down to his position of repose. "You know there is one other thing of which I am very certain."

"Is it that I love you?" Caroline said, leaning down to return his kiss.

"Yes, well, there is that," he said, catching hold of her and flipping their positions.

"Then is it that you will be a father before the summer is done?" Her eyes sparkled as his mouth dropped open, and he pushed up to look at her belly and run a hand over it.

"I had no knowledge of that," he said, leaning down to kiss her. "But I am glad."

"Then what is this thing of which you are so certain?"

He smiled and smoothed her hair back with his right hand before pausing to rest it on her cheek and kissing her once again. "Of this one thing I am very certain — I love you, and I always will."

Happy tears gathered in Caroline's eyes at her good fortune in having secured such a husband. "And you are never wrong about these things?"

He shook his head. "No, and I am even less likely to change my mind."

Before You Go

If you enjoyed this book, be sure to let others know by leaving a review.

~*~*~

Want to know when other books in this series will be available?

You can always know what's new with my books by subscribing to my mailing list.

(There will, of course, be a thank you gift for joining because I think my readers are awesome!)

Book News from Leenie Brown

(bit.ly/LeenieBBookNews)

~*~*~

Turn the page to read an excerpt from another one of Leenie's books

One Winter's Eve Excerpt

If you enjoy stories where Caroline is transformed, you will enjoy One Winter's Eve. This story is the second book in my Darcy Family Holidays collection and features Caroline coming up against and falling in love with another set-in-his-ways sort of fellow named Colonel Fitzwilliam. Below is a short excerpt from the first chapter.

FROM CHAPTER 1

Caroline eyed the man next to the fire as she entered the room.

"Did you find them?" Louisa asked her sister.

Caroline, who had gone in search of a particular pair of gloves about which she had been telling Georgiana, turned her eyes from the colonel and smiled as brilliantly as she could for her sister.

"They were in my small bag in my room, just as I suspected. Are they not just the softest leather, Georgiana?" she asked as she placed them on the table where her brother, Hurst, Louisa, and Georgiana were playing. She had bowed out of playing to make the trip to her room to find the gloves — a trip on which she had discovered more than just those gloves. She had also discovered how a particular gentleman viewed her. She stole a glance at the colonel.

Georgiana placed her hand of cards on the table and slipped on one glove. "They are deliciously soft," she said as she bent her fingers and extended them. "And you said you found them at Harding's?"

"Indeed, I did." Caroline was pleased that her selection of an accessory met with Georgiana's approval. Georgiana was one of those ladies born to the knowledge of the fashion and finery of the upper class. Caroline had been born with a love of such things, but her mother had not been the sort to take her on extensive shopping trips. Caroline had, however, listened and observed where she could and, recently, had studied the Belle Assemblée as diligently as she had ever studied a French primer or work of Mozart. Fashion was the visible mark of the well-to-do lady. Other accomplishments, no matter how masterfully learned, would pale and possibly never be noticed if a lady's first appearance in society did not inform others of her status.

Therefore, Georgiana's approbation was confirmation to Caroline that her diligence was not in vain. Soon, she might even be accepted readily in society, a fact that would now surely be harder than she had hoped. Being Mrs. Darcy would have assured her a proper reception, but since that gentleman seemed intent on not having her, she would have to look to her own abilities. Oh, she could pursue him until he was married and perhaps even after, but what point would there be in that? It would only make her look as foolish as she felt after being rejected by him.

She sighed as she took the gloves back from Georgiana. She was stuck here in Hertfordshire where the only gentlemen of worth or interest were either betrothed or, her eyes narrowed as she once again looked at the man standing by the fire and the object of her current thoughts, disagreeable. Twaddle, indeed! The correct knowledge of fashion was anything but twaddle! Insufferable man!

"I will have to visit that shop when I return to town," Georgiana said, drawing Caroline's attention back to the group with whom she was sitting.

"I hope to one day return to town," Caroline said with a pointed look at her brother.

"Hurst can take you any time he likes," Bingley replied with a grin. "In fact, after the new year, I might wish to have you gone." His grin grew, and she shook her head.

Married. He was actually going to marry Miss Bennet — and as quickly as possible. Those blasted Bennets! First, Darcy and now, her brother. She folded her gloves together and then unfolded them. Perhaps what she needed to do was observe the Bennets and discover their secrets for taking in a rich gentleman and causing him to fall in love with them. Jane was beautiful, but so were others whom her brother had passed over. There must be a look or manner that Miss Bennet possessed which made her desirable. Miss Elizabeth — Caroline's brows furrowed — was not beautiful or charming. There was nothing Caroline could see that would recommend Elizabeth to Darcy, save for her contrary, teasing opinions. Teasing was not something in which Caroline was well-versed. Jane might be the better of the two sisters to attempt to emulate.

"You are rather quiet, Caroline," Bingley said as the round concluded, and he tossed his cards into a pile in the middle of the table.

"I believe I am fatigued from travel," she lied. What tired her was not travel but the state of her life — her desperately unfortunate life — and the thought of remaining unmarried and being passed from brother to sister and back until she became too feeble to be moved.

"You may retire early if you wish," Bingley said with concern. "You are not unwell, are you?"

"No," Caroline assured him with a smile. "However, if Louisa will not miss me..."

"Of course, I shall miss you, but I am fully capable of seeing to our guests in your absence."

"Very well." Caroline rose as Darcy and his cousin approached, their tête-à-tête apparently at a close. "Then I believe I will retire to my room to read."

"You are leaving?" Richard asked. "We have not even had a chance to speak."

Caroline forced her lips into a tight smile. "I am certain you can make do without my twaddle." She fluttered her lashes and added, "*The Lady of the Lake* awaits," before dipping a shallow curtsey and quitting the room.

Acknowledgements

There are always many who play some part in the creation of a story. There are some who have read it as I was writing and listened while I worked out a plot point. and others who I suspect will never read it. And so, I would like to say *thank you* to Zoe, Rose, Ben, and Kyle. I feel blessed through your help, support, and understanding.

I have not listed my dear husband in the above group because, to me, he deserves his own special thank you, for without his somewhat pushy insistence that I start sharing my writing, none of my writing goals and dreams would have been met.

Leenie B Books

You can find all of Leenie's books at this link
bit.ly/LeenieBBooks
where you can explore the collections below

~*~

Other Pens, Mansfield Park

~*~

Touches of Austen

~*~

Dash of Darcy and Companions Collection

~*~

Marrying Elizabeth Series

~*~

Sweet Possibilities and Sweet Extras

~*~

Willow Hall Romances

~*~

The Choices Series

~*~

Darcy Family Holidays

~*~

Darcy and... An Austen-Inspired Collection

~*~

Nature's Fury and Delights (A Sweet Regency Novelettes Series)

~*~

Teatime Tales Novelettes Collection

About the Author

Leenie Brown has always been a girl with an active imagination, which, while growing up, was both an asset, providing many hours of fun as she played out stories, and a liability, when her older sister and aunt would tell her frightening tales. At one time, they had her convinced Dracula lived in the trunk at the end of the bed she slept in when visiting her grandparents!

Although it has been years since she cowered in her bed in her grandparents' basement, she still has an imagination which occasionally runs away with her, and she feeds it now as she did then — by reading!

Her heroes, when growing up, were authors, and the worlds they painted with words were (and still are) her favourite playgrounds! Now, as an adult, she spends much of her time in the Regency world, playing with the characters from her favourite Jane Austen novels and those of her own creation.

When she is not traipsing down a trail in an attempt to keep up with her imagination, Leenie resides in the beautiful province of Nova Scotia with her two sons and her very own Mr. Brown (a wonderful mix of all the best of Darcy, Bingley, and Edmund with a healthy dose of the teasing Mr. Tilney and just a dash of the scolding Mr. Knightley).

Connect with Leenie

E-mail:

LeenieBrownAuthor@gmail.com

Facebook:

www.facebook.com/LeenieBrownAuthor

Blog:

leeniebrown.com

Patreon:

https://www.patreon.com/LeenieBrown

Subscribe to Leenie's Mailing List:

Book News from Leenie Brown

(bit.ly/LeenieBBookNews)

www.ingramcontent.com/pod-product-compliance
Lightning Source LLC
LaVergne TN
LVHW010839120826
845149LV00017B/3313

* 9 7 8 1 9 8 9 4 1 0 7 2 1 *